RITA & RALPH'S

WRITTEN BY **Carmen Agra Deedy**

SCHOLASTIC PRESS

ROTTEN DAY

ILLUSTRATED BY Pete Oswald

NEW YORK

In two little houses,

on two little hills,

lived two best friends.

Every morning, Rita and Ralph would

open their doors,

step outside,

close their doors,

and run . . .

. . . down the hill,   and up the hill,

and down the hill,   and up the hill.

They'd meet under the apple tree and high-five,

pinkie-shake,

do a cha-cha-cha,

play zombie tag,

and make daisy chains.

Then one day . . .

they played a *new* game:

Sticks and Stones.

. . . down the hill,   and up the hill,

and down the hill,   and up the hill.

They opened their doors,

raced inside,

and closed their doors.

Rita was mad.

And Ralph was . . . sorry.

So Ralph opened the door,

stepped outside,

and closed the door.

It was a hundred years to Rita's house.

But she was his best friend.

So Ralph went . . .

down the hill, and up the hill, and down the hill, and up the hill,

and down the hill,

and up the hill,

and down the hill,

aaaaand up the hill.

The long walk made Ralph

a smidge grumpy.

"I'M SORRY!" he barked.

But he

didn't sound

one bit sorry.

So Rita did NOT

open the door.

"Grrrrrrr,"
said Ralph.
And off

he stomped . . .

. . . down the hill, and up the hill, and down the hill, and up the hill, and down the hill, and up the hill, and down the hill, aaaaand up the hill.

He opened the door,

stepped inside,

and closed the door.

Now Ralph was mad.

And Rita was . . . *kinda* sorry.

So she opened the door,

stepped outside,

closed the door,

and ran . . .

. . . down the hill, and up the hill, and down the hill, and up the hill,

and down the hill,

and up the hill,

and down the hill,

aaaaand up the hill.

As she ran,

she thought about Ralph.

And that rock.

Just thinking about it

made her mad

all over again.

"I WANT MY PINECONE BACK!"

she shouted.

Ralph opened the door,

and closed the door.

And Rita tromped . . .

down the hill, and up the hill, and down the hill, and up the hill,

and down the hill,

and up the hill,

and down the hill,

aaaaand up the hill.

She opened her door,

marched inside,

and slammed the door.

Now Rita was mad.

And Ralph was mad.

And Rita was sad.

And Ralph was sad.

And in two little houses on two little hills, no one slept a wink.

It had been a rotten day.

Just when it seemed

nothing would be right again,

it was a new day.

Rita and Ralph

opened their doors,

stepped outside,

closed their doors,

and went . . .

. . . down the hill,   and up the hill,

and down the hill,   and up the hill.

"I'm sorry!" said Rita.

"I'm sorrier!" said Ralph.

And they meant it.

They did a high five,

and a pinkie shake,

and a cha-cha-cha,

and played zombie tag,

and made daisy chains.

Because best friends *always* find a way . . .

. . . to meet in the middle.

101 THINGS
TO BUILD
with a little help
from your friends

Note from the Author

Most of us have said and done things we regret. Nothing feels worse, however, than hurting a friend. Breaking things takes little effort; mending them takes time, humility, and a heap of trips up and down the hills of reconciliation.

This story, inspired by the classic hand game, "Mr. Wiggle & Mr. Waggle," may be read aloud with the accompanying hand gestures on this page. You may even want to add a few of your own!

  1. In two little houses on two little hills

 2. They opened the door

 3. They stepped outside

 4. And they closed the door

  5. They went down the hill

  6. They went up the hill

 7. And they met in the middle

LIBRARY OF CONGRESS CATALOGING-IN-PUBLICATION DATA
Names: Deedy, Carmen Agra, author. | Oswald, Pete, illustrator.
Title: Rita and Ralph's rotten day / by Carmen Agra Deedy;
illustrated by Pete Oswald. Description: First edition. | New York :
Scholastic Press, 2020. | Summary: Rita and Ralph live on
neighboring hills and they are best friends, until a silly accident
while goofing around ends up with both of them angry and
unhappy—and they both need to find a way to heal the break in their
relationship. • Identifiers: LCCN 2018060396 | ISBN 9781338216387
Subjects: LCSH: Best friends—Juvenile fiction.
| Friendship—Juvenile fiction. | Anger—Juvenile fiction.
| Apologizing—Juvenile fiction. | • CYAC: Best friends—Fiction.
| Friendship—Fiction. | Anger—Fiction. | Apologizing—Fiction.
Classification: LCC PZ7.D3587 Ri 2020 | DDC [E]—dc23

10 9 8 7 6 5 4 3 2 1   20 21 22 23 24

Printed in China   38 • First edition, March 2020

For my
grandchildren,
Ruby,
Sam,
Grace,
Brady,
and
Chloe.
— C.D.

For
Nini
— P.O.

Special thanks — to Sherry Norfolk,
educator, storyteller,
and most generous friend. — C.D.

Pete Oswald's illustrations were rendered digitally using gouache watercolor textures.
The text type was set in Futura Medium. • The display type was set in Khaki Std 1.
The book was printed on 157 gsm Golden Sun Matte and bound at RR Donnelley Asia.
Production was overseen by Catherine Weening. • Manufacturing was supervised by Shannon Rice.
The book was art directed and designed by Marijka Kostiw, and edited by Dianne Hess.